Postcards from • Postales desde

CHICAGO

Traveling with Anna • De viaje con Ana

★ Laura Crawford ★

To Brook + Megan
Miller-

Enjoy your journies!
Love,
Laura Crawford

To Kim Corcoran

Text Copyright © 2008 Laura Crawford
Illustration and Translation Copyright © 2008 Raven Tree Press

Crawford, Laura.
Illustrations by Bonnie Adamson
Book Design by Amanda Chavez

Postcards from Chicago / written by Laura Crawford ; translated by Eida de la Vega =
Postales desde Chicago / escrito por Laura Crawford ; traducción al español de Eida
de la Vega — 1st ed. — McHenry, IL : Raven Tree Press, 2008.
       p. ; cm.
       Text in English and Spanish.

       Summary: Join Anna in her travel adventures to a favorite city
of the United States, Chicago, IL. Child writes postcards home
to friends with facts about historical and tourist sites.

       ISBN: 978–0–9795477–4–4 Hardcover
       ISBN: 978–0–9795477–5–1 Paperback

1. People & Places/United States — Juvenile fiction. 2. Biographical/United States —
Juvenile fiction. 3. People & Places/United States — Juvenile non fiction.
4. Bilingual books — English and Spanish. 5. [Spanish language materials—books.]
I. Title II. Title: Postales desde Chicago.

Library of Congress Control Number: 2007939496

Printed in Taiwan
10 9 8 7 6 5 4 3 2 1
First Edition

Raven Tree Press
A Division of Delta Publishing Company
www.raventreepress.com

Hi! My name is Anna. My family is taking a trip to Chicago, Illinois! Dad calls it The Windy City. Some people think the name Chicago came from an Indian word meaning "stinky onions." Isn't that funny? I'm glad I saved my money so I can buy postcards for my family and friends.

¡Hola! Me llamo Anna. Mi familia va a viajar a Chicago, en Illinois. Papá le dice "La ciudad de los vientos". Hay gente que piensa que el nombre Chicago proviene de una palabra india que significa "cebollas apestosas". ¿Verdad que es gracioso? Me alegra haber ahorrado dinero para poder comprar postales para mi familia y amigos.

3

Dear Grandma and Grandpa,

I visited the Field Museum of Natural History and saw the fossils of Sue, the biggest Tyrannosaurus Rex. I felt so tiny! They paid over 8 million dollars for the dinosaur. We saw a lot of different dinosaurs. On the way to the hotel, we drove down Lakeshore Drive to see Lake Michigan. There were boats everywhere!

Love, Anna

★ Sue was named after the woman who discovered her bones in South Dakota.

★ There are life-sized Egyptian tombs.

★ Lake Michigan is one of 5 bodies of water called the Great Lakes.

4

Field Museum of Natural History

⭐ A Sue la llamaron así por la mujer que descubrió sus huesos en Dakota del Sur.

⭐ Hay tumbas egipcias de tamaño real.

⭐ El lago Michigan es uno de los cinco Grandes Lagos.

Sears Tower

6

Hola Manuel,

Today we went to the top of the Sears Tower. It is one of the tallest buildings in the world. Each year there's a race to the top- it's 2,109 stairs! I'd have to train for months! A robotic machine cleans the 16,000 windows. Mom wanted to take the robot home with us!

Hasta luego, Anna ♡

⭐ The Sears Tower sways slightly on windy days.

⭐ The elevators are some of the fastest in the world.

⭐ You can see Michigan, Wisconsin, Illinois and Indiana.

⭐ Las Torres Sears oscilan un poco en días ventosos.

⭐ Sus elevadores son unos de los más rápidos del mundo.

⭐ Puedes ver Michigan, Wisconsin, Illinois e Indiana.

7

Dear Jill and Kim,

You would've loved the Shedd Aquarium. The beluga whales squeaked and splashed us! The penguins looked like little torpedoes zooming through the water. When I grow up, I'm going to be a diver that goes into the tank. I'd be a little nervous about that nurse shark, though.

Bye for now, Anna ♡

⭐ The Shedd Aquarium is one of the largest indoor aquariums.

⭐ It has over 22,000 animals.

⭐ The Amazon exhibit has anacondas, giant spiders and poisonous frogs.

Shedd Aquarium

⭐ El acuario Shed es uno de los acuarios bajo techo más grandes del mundo.

⭐ Tiene más de 22,000 animales.

⭐ La exhibición del Amazonas tiene anacondas, arañas gigantes y ranas venenosas.

Magnificent
Mile

Dear Jackson,

I had a wonderful time on the Magnificent Mile. It has over 400 stores. Mom screamed when we saw Oprah Winfrey walking down Michigan Avenue! She gave us her autograph. Thousands of people visit the 'Mag Mile' to see the beautiful holiday decorations.

Miss you, Anna ♡

★ The John Hancock Building and Water Tower Place are on this street.

★ Marshall Fields was the first department store.

★ People come to see the gardens that line the street.

    ★ El edificio John Hancock y la Water Tower Place están en esta calle.

    ★ Marshall Fields fue la primera tienda por departamentos.

    ★ La gente viene a ver los jardines que decoran la calle.

Dear Mrs. Johnson and Class,

Today we saw the Old Water Tower. It's one of the few buildings to survive The Great Chicago Fire. Some think the fire started when a dairy cow kicked a lantern over in Mrs. O'Leary's barn, but that's probably not true. The fire burned for 2 days because of the wooden buildings. I'll tell you more when I get home.

Be home soon, Anna ♡

★ After the fire of 1871, people built with cement and bricks.

★ Dry weather and wind helped the fire grow. Rain helped put it out.

★ It took only 5 years to rebuild the city of Chicago.

★ Después del fuego de 1871, la gente empezó a construir con cemento y ladrillos.

★ El clima seco y el viento contribuyeron a que el fuego se extendiera. La lluvia ayudó a extinguirlo.

★ La ciudad de Chicago se reconstruyó en cinco años.

Old Water Tower

Navy Pier

★ The first ferris wheel was made here in 1893.

★ Navy Pier was used for training in World War II.

★ The Navy is one of the 5 armed services of the United States.

Ricardo y Maria,

Wow, Chi-town is exciting. Navy Pier has a huge ferris wheel. I loved the barnyard area. The giant insects and plants made me feel like a little bug! There is a huge screen to watch movies. We even got to see fireworks over the water tonight. What a day!

Sinceramente, Anna ♡

⭐ La primera rueda de la fortuna se hizo aquí en 1893.

⭐ El muelle de la Marina se usaba como lugar de entrenamiento durante la II Guerra Mundial.

⭐ La Marina es uno de los cinco cuerpos armados de Los Estados Unidos.

Dear Natalie,

Today we took a boat tour of the Chicago River. We passed the business district called "The Loop." In 1890, they reversed the direction of the Chicago River by building a series of locks that made the river flow the other way. It sent the pollution away from Lake Michigan. I didn't know they could do that.

See you later, Anna ♡

⭐ The Chicago River is dyed green for St. Patrick's Day.
⭐ Chicago has more movable bridges than any city in the world.
⭐ The first drawbridge was built in Chicago.

Chicago River

⭐ El día de San Patricio tiñen de verde el río Chicago.

⭐ Chicago tiene más puentes levadizos que cualquier otra ciudad del mundo.

⭐ El primer puente levadizo se construyó en Chicago.

Soldier Field

⭐ It was named in honor of the soldiers of World War I.

⭐ It opened on October 9, 1954, the anniversary of the Chicago Fire.

⭐ Soldier Field is located on Lake Shore Drive.

Dear Pam,

Dad was so happy today because we went to Soldier Field. This is the stadium where the Chicago Bears play football. Everyone was wearing blue and orange. The stadium was rebuilt in 2003. Now it looks like a flipped over spaceship. I've never seen a building like this before!

Take care, Anna ♡

⭐ Se le nombró en honor a los soldados de la I Guerra Mundial.

⭐ Se inauguró el 9 de octubre de 1954, el aniversario del incendio de Chicago.

⭐ Soldier Field está localizado en Lake Shore Drive.

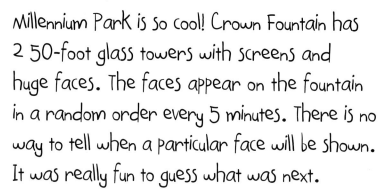

Carmela,

Millennium Park is so cool! Crown Fountain has 2 50-foot glass towers with screens and huge faces. The faces appear on the fountain in a random order every 5 minutes. There is no way to tell when a particular face will be shown. It was really fun to guess what was next.

Cariños, Anna ♡

★ A millennium is 1,000 years. This park was dedicated in the year 2000.

★ The faces on the fountain spray water from their mouths.

★ The plants in this park are all native to Illinois.

★ Un milenio son 1,000 años. Este parque se inauguró en el año 2000.

★ Las caras en la fuente sueltan agua por la boca.

★ Todas las plantas de este parque son nativas de Illinois.

20

Millennium Park

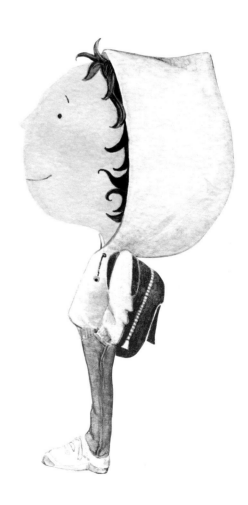

⭐ European suits of armor are on display here.

⭐ *American Gothic* by Grant Wood is on display.

⭐ Several pieces of furniture by Frank Lloyd Wright are here.

Paco y Paula,

The Art Institute was amazing! Mom loved Claude Monet's paintings. I liked Seurat's *A Sunday at La Grande Jatte*. It's a pattern of little dots called pointillism. When the White Sox won the World Series, someone put baseball hats on the lions that are on the front steps of the Art Institute! Isn't that funny?

Te extraño, Anna ♡

★ Aquí se exhiben armaduras europeas.

★ Tambien se exhibe el cuadro de Grant Wood, *Gótico Americano*.

★ Hay varios muebles diseñados por Frank Lloyd Wright.

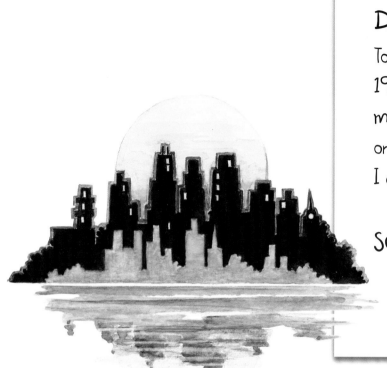

Dear Larry and Jackie,

Today we saw the Wrigley Building. It was built in 1920 by the Wrigley family. They were famous for making chewing gum. The building has huge clocks on all 4 sides. There is no reason to be late here. I didn't need my watch all day.

See ya later, Anna ♡

★ The Wrigley family owned the Chicago Cubs.
★ The building is covered with 250,000 white tiles.
★ It was modeled after a building in Spain.

★ La familia Wrigley era dueña del equipo los Cachorros de Chicago.
★ El edificio está cubierto con 250,000 mosaicos blancos.
★ Tomaron como modelo un edificio de España.

Wrigley Building

Buckingham Fountain

⭐ Over 60 restaurants provide all types of food for The Taste.

⭐ The "L" is short for elevated or above the ground.

⭐ Chicago is the home of the second elevated train system. New York had the first.

Mrs. Hernandez,

Today was great! The Taste of Chicago is a 10 day festival in Grant Park. Chefs cook food right on the street! We sat by Buckingham Fountain and ate lunch. Mom's Chicago style pizza was delicious. Dad and I tried alligator. We also rode the 'L', an elevated train. It was so loud and shaky.

Sinceramente, Anna ♡

⭐ Más de 60 restaurantes proveen todo tipo de comida para El Sabor.

⭐ "L" es la abreviatura que se usa para elevado o por encima del suelo.

⭐ Chicago es el hogar del segundo sistema de trenes elevados. Nueva York tuvo el primero.

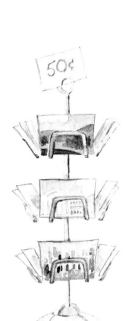

Margarita,

Today we went to the Adler Planetarium. We sat in a dark theater and looked at star patterns on the ceiling. I found the Big Dipper! We also saw a huge sundial outside behind the museum. That is how they used to tell time. It was so cool!

Me despido por ahora, Anna ♡

- ★ Visitors can go outside in the evening to see real constellations.
- ★ Adler hosts a night when families can sleep in the museum.
- ★ Visitors can look through a very powerful telescope.

Adler Planetarium

★ Los visitantes pueden salir por la noche para ver constelaciones de verdad.

★ Hay una noche en que las familias pueden dormir en Adler.

★ Los visitantes pueden mirar a través de un poderoso telescopio.

Polar Bear at the
Lincoln Park Zoo

30

Dear Uncle Frank,

Today was awesome! We went to the Lincoln Park Zoo. It's the oldest free zoo in the country. The polar bears were hilarious. They splashed and swam around. Dad liked the 2 baby apes in the primate house that were throwing straw at each other! Mom loved the cute little puffins! I bought a stuffed polar bear to remember this day forever.

Love, Anna ♡

★ The zoo started with a gift of 2 swans from New York's Central Park.

★ In 1874, they bought a bear cub for 10 dollars.

★ The zoo is known for helping endangered species.

   ★ El zoológico se abrió con un regalo de 2 cisnes del Parque Central de Nueva York.

   ★ En 1874, compraron un cachorro de oso por 10 dólares.

   ★ El zoológico es conocido por ayudar a las especies en peligro de extinción.

I had a wonderful time in The City of Big Shoulders. I learned so much about Chicago! I can't wait to go back!

Lo pasé de maravilla en "La ciudad de las espaldas grandes". ¡Aprendí mucho sobre Chicago! ¡Estoy impaciente por volver!